50 smart, easy and effectve ideas to

BOOST YOUR BUSINESS TODAY

by Michelle Kabele

Introduction

How's business? No matter how you're doing, it could be better. Sometimes, you just need some fresh ideas, a little inspiration, or maybe just a sharp kick to jump-start your success. Improving your business doesn't require a hefty advertising budget. You don't have to make drastic changes in your business plan, staff, or product line. In this guide, you'll discover dozens of practical tips to increase your sales, build customer loyalty, uncover new customers and sales opportunities, and establish yourself as a vita resource as the thought leader with the answers. *50 Smart, Easy, and Effective Ideas To Boost Your Business Today* will show you how to ...

- Meet — and exceed — your customers' needs

- Build your reputation as a knowledgeable expert

- Expand your reach in the marketplace

- Use the Internet for maximum benefit

- Improve your business planning to deliver measurable results

- Create promotional opportunities that will drive sales

- Gain more sales from your existing customers

- ...and much, much more!

Work your way through this list and choose ten ideas to get started. Give yourself daily and weekly goals and measure your progress. Once you've tried all 50 ideas, revisit those that provided the best results. Keep repeating them. As for the ideas that didn't work for you, maybe you can give them another try, with a slightly different approach. Or use these ideas as a springboard to launch new ones that will help you reach your goals and objectives.

Now, open up your notebook and your mind, and prepare to achieve greater success!

Get organized.

1. SET UP A SYSTEM FOR KEEPING NOTES.

Every day, you're probably jotting down notes here and there — reminders of things you need to do for clients, ideas to pursue, and questions or problems that you want to answer. If you don't have a system for organizing your notes, you could be missing out on opportunities to build your reputation as a follow-through resource. And you are undoubtedly missing opportunities for capturing more sales, improving your customer relationships, and boosting your profitability! Can you see why this is Idea #1? Whether you set up a system of folders or a bulletin board with categories like "To Do", "Return Calls", "Get More Info", and "Schedule Appointment", make it easily accessible so you can make notes after every phone call and include messages from your email. It doesn't matter what you use — a day planner, smartphone, computer — just as long as you use it faithfully!

2. USE YOUR NEW NOTE SYSTEM.

It seems crazy to include this step, but there can be a huge gap between *starting* up a system and actually *using* it on a daily basis. Enter and review your notes. Check your notes daily. Make a "To Do" list of action items, such as people to call, people to email, research, etc. And check off each item as you accomplish it.

Be sure to add and file new notes to keep your system up-to-date!

3. USE A POST CARD TO REFRESH
YOUR CUSTOMER DATABASE.

Email addresses change daily. People move on to another job or simply change their server. Whatever the reason, you might not be privy to the changes if you don't make an effort to ask. Send a post card to your database twice a year to let them know you want to remain connected. Invite them to go to your site to confirm their email address, and provide an incentive to do so (e.g., register for a giveaway). Be sure to specify "Change Service Requested" under the return address on your post card so the bad addresses (undeliverable as addressed, moved, out of business) come back to you. It's worth the small price you pay to get them back. Snail-mail a post card to update

4. CATEGORIZE YOUR DATABASE.

Look at your database, the one that has all the great purchasing notes on each client (see Idea #5). A great, big database can be impressive but isn't particularly useful. You need to be able to categorize your customers by segments. Make sure you have fields with total annual sales, so you can break out your top performers and those lesser-spending customers who need a nudge. Segment them according to the types of products they buy to make your target marketing a bulls-eye. Be sure you can have fields that identify your customers by specific industries, job categories, locations, etc. Then you can pull up a report that shows where you larger groups are, and where you have opportunities for growth.

5. UPDATE THE SALES NOTES ON YOUR DATABASE.

Your database is more than a list of customers and addresses. Think of it as your customer treasure chest?. You should make notes of who bought what and when. Can you sort your list according to who bought a particular product so you can them know about updates or accessories that go with it? Look at Amazon. They send notices to customers with recommendations based on what you have viewed or purchased from them: "Customers who bought this also bought this." Use your database to keep in touch with your buyers. They'll love the fact that you know more about them than their bottom line dollar value!

6. OUTLINE YOUR MARKETING ACTION PLAN.

Take two hours each quarter to work on your MAP (marketing action plan) for success. How do you plan to get from Point A (the here and now) to Point B (meeting your goals)? What steps are you going to take to achieve those goals? What specific tasks will be required, and when will each one be implemented? If you're planning an e-newsletter, when do you want to send it? (Advice: Tuesdays and Wednesdays are the best days.) What promotions do you have in mind? When are you going to launch (and end) them? Pick a monthly theme; outline what you want to do to reach your customers with the theme; and then prioritize the most important ones, according to a scale like this: crucial; important; useful but not important; or just fun ideas worth exploring. Once you've detailed the necessary tasks, assign owners and deadlines to each action. You'll be surprised at how much you can get completed with an actionable list that's focused — not to mention the results that you'll achieve from these integrated actions! Send this "punch list" to everyone involved, at the beginning and end of each week.

7. MAKE A GOALS BOARD.

Here's an easy idea that will keep you focused on meeting your primary objectives. Hang a dry erase board in your office. Mark off spaces for short-term (weekly, monthly) and long-term (quarterly, annual) goals. Be sure that they are measurable. For example, don't set a goal of "adding more customers". Set a goal of "adding 10 new customers next month". By making them measurable, there will never be any question about whether you succeeded in meeting them. Give yourself goals in every category. Make a list of five things you can do today to get closer to achieving those desires. If, for example, you want to add 10 new clients in one month, how many calls do you need to make in one day? What will it take to stay on task and meet — or beat! — those goals?

Be a better communicator.

8. CALL FIVE CUSTOMERS.

Your best source for new sales and market knowledge and business trends comes from your existing customers. Today, pick five — any five. Whether they have ordered recently or have been absent for six months or more. Call each one. Ask about their business. What are they working on? What's selling well? What isn't? Identify a need that you can address (either right then and there, or do a little homework and get back to them). Find a problem you can solve. The goal of these calls is to build your reputation among your customers as a valuable, go-to resource and not so much about making an immediate sale.

9. SURVEY YOUR CUSTOMERS.

If you want to know what your customers need, want, and aren't getting, ask them! Believe me, they want to be heard. Call five of your regular customers today and ask what they would like to see added or improved on your site. "How can our site be more valuable and useful to you?" Then call five customers who have fallen off your radar and ask them what you can do to bring them back! They will all appreciate your earnest interest.

10. REACT TO YOUR CUSTOMERS' FEEDBACK.

After you've made the effort to call your customers and find out where you can improve, make the necessary changes immediately. Make the adjustments to your site, based on the feedback from your customers. This effort showcases your sincere interest in their feedback and builds on the relationship.

11. SHARE YOUR IMPROVEMENTS
WITH YOUR CUSTOMERS.

Once you've risen to the challenge, call those customers who offered feedback and let them know that you listened and responded. Let them know what you've done to better meet their needs. And be sure to thank them for their candor in helping you to serve them better. Then, send an email blast to all of your customers with a link to the "new and improved" sections of your website where you've posted those changes.

12. THANK YOUR CUSTOMERS.

The best link to new customers is your satisfied customer. Go through your database right now and find your best customers. Thank them for their loyalty by sending a personal note, gift, or "customer appreciation" offer. Don't wait until the holidays to do this because your appreciation will get lost in the crowd of holiday gift-giving. And whatever you do, be sure to extend it as a personal message, not a mass mailing, so that your VIPs know exactly how "VI" they are!

Become a trusted advisor.

13. EMAIL AN INTERESTING LINK TO YOUR CUSTOMERS.

How often do you come across an article that offers great insight or find a blog that makes incredible sense? Send out an email blast to your customers and include the hyperlink. Your customers will appreciate that you are looking after their interests and not solely focused on always making a sale. By sharing helpful information, you transform yourself from just another vendor into a knowledgeable, attentive, and helpful resource.

14. SEND YOUR CUSTOMERS AND PROSPECTS A MONTHLY BUSINESS TIP.

Build on your reputation as a thought leader by sharing a monthly nugget with your database new, existing, and prospective customers. Use email or snail-mail a post card. Just keep it simple. Offer an interesting bit of knowledge (such as the one about visitors totally bypassing your home page!). If it's helpful information (no hard selling, please), your customers and prospects will hold on to it and remember where it came from. Plus, they'll actually look forward to getting the next piece from you.

15. TEACH WHAT YOU KNOW.

The Internet has proven that we are a society that is starved for information. People surf the 'Net for information on subjects, products, services, and more. We research our destinations before booking our own flight (after we've checked out all possibilities). We get our news blasts here. So use the insatiable appetite for knowledge and host an evening or one-day class about a topic related to your business. Offer a "how to" for the latest software. Teach students and adults how to make better use of their computer applications. Many community centers or community colleges are looking for course content. Teaching a class will introduce you to people who are interested in what you have to say. Some of them could become customers; others could turn into resources; and you might even find your next superstar employee! (Note: Leaders teach)

16. CONNECT CUSTOMERS TO YOUR COLLABORATION NETWORK.

You learned a valuable lesson in kindergarten: share! Just because you're a big, successful SuperVAR doesn't mean you should forget this! Use your network of proven resources to support your customers. For example, let's say one of your customers needs help in setting up a home computer network and although you don't offer this service, you know someone who does. Bring the two together. You're not giving away a customer to a competition, but you are enhancing your reputation as a knowledgeable, valuable resource who is always ready with a solution. Connecting customers with your network is a great way to build relationships, boost sales, and get referrals!

17. ANSWER A QUESTION ON LINKEDIN.

Go to LinkedIn's "Answers" tab and click on "Answer Questions". Here you'll find a vast array of problems just waiting for the right solution. Step in so you can become a knowledge expert! Some of these are very deep, like "What should a world citizen be like?" or quick fixes: "Can anyone recommend a great computer guy in the Phoenix area?" Tag. You're it. Now it's *your* turn to be the thought leader.

Remember that "network" is an action verb.

18. ATTEND A LOCAL NETWORKING EVENT.

Sure, this is not a new idea, but it's still a good one. I know, you're probably saying that those gatherings are always populated by the same sales people pitching the same products to the same audience. So, nix that mixer! Look for other groups (see Idea #22), possibly in another town so you can broaden your horizons (and customer or resource base). Make a concerted effort to meet new people. Ask them about their business and *listen* intently to their responses. There could be opportunities somewhere in there! Use the event as an information gathering activity rather than actively putting out sales pitches. The sales will come when you uncover those fresh opportunities.

19. PLAN A NETWORKING SESSION.

Create an occasion to bring your customers together where they can gain knowledge, product updates, connections, and ideas for growing their business. Host a breakfast, luncheon, or after-hours cocktail reception (food and drink will also lure them in). Bring in a speaker or host a roundtable discussion on topic of interest to the group. Need some ideas? Ask your customers, "What's keeping you up at night?" "What training would help you grow your business?" Find thought leaders in these subjects. Then be the thoughtful person who brings these leaders together with your customers, who will be very appreciative! And be sure to encourage your customers to bring a friend or colleague so you can continue to grow your network! Or start your own resource network by putting out an invitation to businesses you know and respect. Throw out a discussion topic that will intrigue them, like "How Can We Create Happier Customers?"

20. JOIN A LOCAL BUSINESS ORGANIZATION.

Never underestimate the power of networking within organizations like your local or state Chamber of Commerce, economic development group, or Rotary. Participate in meetings, join committees, attend mixers. Find out if you can use the membership list to promote your ideas and your business. Members are often more likely to chose the services of another member so the investment of your time can come back with sales and business contacts. Plus, more visibility in your community is always a good thing!

21. JOIN LINKEDIN.

This social networking site is for business professionals only. You won't find wild videos and crazy photos. The objective of LinkedIn is to help you connect with other business professionals via the Internet. Find resources and sales leads. Build online relationships with thought leaders. LinkedIn is a who's who of savvy pros who understand the vast opportunities of the World Wide Web. It only takes ten minutes to set up your profile. Then you can search for possible connections and start building your network. Be sure to check out Guy Kawasaki's (one of the original Apple guys and the Macintosh marketing maven) blog, "10 Ways to Use LinkedIn." He covers everything from improving your Google PageRank to gauging the health of a company or industry.

22. SEARCH ONLINE FOR GROUPS WITH LIKE INTERESTS.

Once you've established your presence on LinkedIn, you can search the Groups Directory to find gatherings of professionals in all walks of life. If you're interested in reaching out to techno-types, just go to "Search Groups" and type in some key words, like "computers" or "technology" or even "channel marketing" to build your networks. BUT, your connections don't end here! Go to Yahoo! Groups and plug in some search terms to link with groups that aren't linked in to LinkedIn. Dedicate one hour today to searching and joining at least two online groups that match your professional interests. Look for entrepreneurs or marketing gurus. Seek out groups who are expert sales pros. The point is to meet people who can broaden your horizons with great ideas, inspiration, knowledge, insight, and other great motivators!

Learn something new every day.

23. POST A QUESTION ON LINKEDIN.

Since you should, by now, be actively seeking solutions to make your customers view you as a powerful resource and ally in their quest to succeed, a visit to LinkedIn can give you some helpful advice. You can post a question to the LinkedIn community. You can choose the category for your question and zoom in on the right people to give you the best answers. Here's your opportunity to build your own resources in the boundless virtual universe. Remember, you are as good as your network so invest in continually building it!

24. READ!

Successful entrepreneurs will tell you that they are information junkies. They read everything they can — books, magazines, ezines, blogs — to find out what's hot, cool, and brilliant. Go sit in your favorite café and read a magazine, such as Inc, Entrepreneur, or Fast Company to uncover trends, business improvement tips, and other information you might have otherwise overlooked. Get a book on business management, marketing, e-marketing, time management — something that you'd like to learn how to do better. If you're not sure which, check out the readers' ratings and reviews on Amazon.

25. KEEP YOURSELF IN THE KNOW!

Go to buzz.yahoo.com to read what people are talking about. Keep a step ahead of your competitors, colleagues, clients, and peers by checking out this site once a day. Find out what people are talking about online: what news items they're discussing, what videos they're clicking in to watch. You can search buzz topics, post a comment to an item, or just build your knowledge of the latest chat so you can be reinforce your role as the thought leader.

26. GET EXECUTIVE SUMMARIES OF THE BOOKS YOU SHOULD BE READING.

As I've already said, reading is the best way to keep up on trends, techniques, and other bits that contribute to being a successful business owner and resource for your clients. But time is always the most precious commodity these days, so if you can't read, skim! Executive book summaries are the businessperson's version of those good, old Cliff Notes. When you don't have time to read the whole book, look at a summary of the key points and information. You can subscribe to summary services like Soundview and Business Summaries and get your summary in your choice of a print, online, or audio format.

27. USE YOUR TRAVEL TIME WISELY.

Audio books are the best invention since, well, books! Download an audio business book to your computer or mp3 player and listen to it while you're commuting, exercising on the treadmill, or enjoying a little down time on the hammock in the back yard. It's the ultimate in executive multi-tasking! You can borrow audio books on CD from your local library, rent them from services like Simply Audio Books. Jiggerbug, or audiotogo, (via CD or instant download), or build your personal library by purchasing audio books.

28. CHECK OUT THE BUSINESS SERVICES OFFERED BY GOOGLE, MSN, AND YAHOO!

They're not just search engines. These corporations are smart enough to know that they have to do more than direct you to other people's sites. They make money by keeping you engaged in their own website. Yahoo! and Google represent some of the brightest marketing in today's business world. Check out Google Analytics and learn how to get better tracking of your site's visitors. Get automatic alerts when your business name appears on the Internet. Take one hour today and explore the value-added services available on these search engines' sites (a perfect example of these companies implementing Idea #37).

29. TALK TO YOUR VENDORS.

You're not alone in your business. You can — and should — rely on your vendors to support your sales efforts. At least once a quarter, reach out to your vendors and find out what resources, ideas, and promotions they have available for you. Check on additional training to help you sell their products more effectively. Ask about promotions (giveaways, premiums, rebates, bundles) that you can use to boost sales in the upcoming quarter? Regularly visit the dealer page on their website and remind your rep to keep you informed of all these opportunities. Also find out if they are advertising locally where your contact information can be featured. And be *sure* that you are listed as an authorized dealer on their website and that your link is featured there.

Master the Internet.

30. BUILD YOUR WEBSITE IN A DAY.

If you haven't already developed a website for your business, do it! You're in a world where it's expected that every business has an online presence. Even if you're not trying to find clients outside your local or regional territory, those that you do have will see you as out of touch if you don't have a site. And it's so easy to do, with programs such as iWeb (which comes already installed on the Mac) and Web Page Maker (free download for the PC). The programs guide you through the process of building your site, one step at a time. The templates make it incredibly easy to get your site up and running, literally in one hour! You can incorporate photos, set up a blog (a great tool on its own!), and even use Google Maps to show people how to find you. It's never been easier to make a professional looking website on your own.

31. BLOG.

Blogging isn't new, but it's hot, hot, hot! You can spend 10 to 15 minutes a day commenting about a new product (breakthrough or bomb), a business news item, or a problem you solved for your customer. Anything more than a paragraph is overkill! It will show your customers that you're up on (and comfortable with) this cool communication tool. And if you blog regularly (three to five times a week), it will also improve your site's rankings on search engines. You can also set up a subscriber opt-in so that interested readers automatically get your blog emailed to them — a regular reminder of your thought leadership! It's easy to add a blogging page to your site. If you use iWeb or Web Page Maker, the feature is built right in. You can also get free blog hosting at Wordpress.com or Blogger.com, or inexpensive hosting (with some cool benefits) at Typepad.com. Blog regularly — at least three times a week! It shouldn't take no than about 15 minutes to dash off and post a blog. And, when you're feeling particularly eloquent, write several blogs and stash them to upload later, when time is less available.

32. OPTIMIZE YOUR WEBSITE.

Search engine optimization is the best way to ensure that customers can find you online! SEO cranks up the effectiveness of your site by making it more pleasing to the search engine spiders that crawl around looking for the best match to organic searches. Regularly refreshed content (e.g., blogs, product updates) and plenty of relevant links (emphasis on "relevant") will help to boost your page ranking. A little advice here: The search engines are constantly adjusting their algorithms for SEO so this is not a task you should tackle without experience. This Great Idea requires that you seek out an SEO specialist to optimize your site on a monthly basis.

33. ADD A "LATEST NEWS" SECTION TO YOUR SITE.

Don't assume that your home page is the one and only portal into your website. Most people come at your site sideways (linking to an interior or landing page) and don't even see the home page! (Google Analytics, Idea #28, is a great tool for tracking this movement). When they come, and wherever they arrive, you need to be sure they can easily find the latest news (special promotions, upcoming events, product updates, press releases). Feature a link to "Latest News" on every page. And, please, be vigilant about keeping this page fresh.

If a visit comes to your "Latest News" and finds an outdated software version or an "upcoming" event that has passed, you'll appear lazy. Once a week, go back to this page and be sure it's up-to-date.

34. PUBLISH YOUR SUCCESSES.

Don't be shy when you've done a good job. It's okay to toot your horn. Tell your customers how you've solved a problem for someone. Let them know when you've received an honor, award, certification, or other recognition. Sharing these victories — small or large — helps both you and your customers. Your "success story" may spark an inquiry from a new or existing customer who has similar problem and hasn't been able to find a solution. So write it up and put it on your site! Send out an email blast with an abbreviated version and a link to that page on your site. And, in your email, invite them to submit their success stories to share with your group: "What's working great for you right now? We'd love to hear from you!"

35. SUBMIT YOUR SUCCESS STORY TO AN ARTICLE DIRECTORY.

Article directories or banks gather informative articles and make them available to the world at large. If you've ever done an organic search to learn about a topic, you've probably come across some of these sites. IdeaMarketers.com, articledashboard.com, and ezinearticles.com are a few examples. You can use these sites to promote your knowledge by writing a brief article (usually 500 to 1,000 words) on a very specific topic. The directories welcome interesting articles that offer tips and ideas (e.g., "10 Ways to…" "The 25 Hottest…" and "The 7 Best…."). It's easy to submit your article to these sites; check out their submission criteria because it varies according to the site. But once your article is posted, you'll find that other directories will pick it up and post the piece on their sites as well, so you get the viral advantage here. If you're groaning at the idea of writing an article, hire a freelancer to do it for you. For as little as $50, you can have someone ghostwrite a 500-word piece for you. Not sure where to find a writer? Go to guru.com or elance.com.

36. RECORD A PODCAST.

A podcast is an audio recording that can be downloaded from your site to a visitor's computer or mp3 player. Have a salesperson inter-view about a new trend or product that your customers would like to know about. Record an interview with a customer who has a great success story (see Idea #34) — preferably one you helped to create! A podcast can be as short as five minutes or as long as 30 minutes (any longer than that and you might lose your listener). You can record your podcast right from your computer (if you have that capa-bility) and can even make it into a video with your computer's built-in camera. Unlike the old days, the quality is not the big issue here. It's the timeliness and value of the message. All the world is creating user-generated content (thus, the YouTube phenomenon) so jump on this idea right away! It takes less than one hour and you can deliver your podcasts as an RSS feed (i.e., automatically sent to people who subscribe to it), on iTunes, or from your own website. All you need are the ideas and one hour. right on your desk.)

Explore your promotional brilliance.

37. THINK OF A BRILLIANT VALUE-ADD IDEA
TO BETTER SERVE YOUR CUSTOMERS.

What would make your customers stand up and take a fresh look at your business? The broad answer is: exceed their expectations. Give them something that they will value without charging them for it. Add convenience to their lives. Look at Best Buy's Geek Squad and the Apple Store's Genius Bar. The powers that be recognized that if they are *selling* computer equipment, then why not capture the added revenue by offering the convenience of in-store technical support? Brilliant! What can you do to tempt your customers with something of value that will provide a good ROI? Can you in-source a service, like The Geek Squad for Best Buy? Are there products that aren't moving because they haven't been tried? If so, consider bundling it with better movers. It's not going to cost your customers if you try giving them more than they ask for. But if you don't try, you will likely lose them to those competitors who are taking this advice. And you'll miss out on the priceless value of that viral word-of-mouth advertising that goes along with exceeding your customers' expectations! Value-adds are not an expense but an investment in building brand loyalty.

What about the value you create with walking/talking endorsements for your service and hardware. Brand loyalty is built through these "services". Have you ever called Best Buy service when your TV goes out in the middle of the night? You reach a live person…and get a fast response! Or, if you're trying to resolve something on the computer – go right into the Apple store and they'll teach you how to use the computer and a variety of software. Sure, they could charge you – but would you switch computer brands with that type of service? Walking, talking word-of-mouth advertising delivers the #1 most trusted source for referrals and influence on purchases – how much is that worth to your brand?

38. DONATE A DOOR PRIZE TO A BUSINESS NETWORKING EVENT.

The organizers of these events are always looking for door prizes in order to entice more participants. What can you donate that will appeal to the attendees, promote your company, and reflect your savvy approach? Don't make the mistake of giving a product that has been collecting dust on the shelves. These events aren't flea markets! Put up a brand new trinket that many of the people in the audience haven't tried yet. Now they'll know you have the latest, greatest stuff! If you are service-oriented, give them a sample of your most unique service so that, again, the attendees get the word about your commitment to their deepest desires.

39. USE YOUR IMPROVED DATABASE.

After completing Idea #5, go back to your updated database and look for opportunities to make a sale. Is there a new version of a particular software program or hardware that they should know about? Is their system out of date? Is the manufacturer offering a new bundle, special promotion, or webinar to help customers make the most of their purchase? Where are the noticeable gaps in your selling cycles and customers' buying habits? Play detective here and look for the clues to improving your sales. Spend an hour today focused exclusively on exploring your database, away from distractions.

I guarantee that, if you examine it closely enough, you will find opportunities.

40. CREATE A PROMOTION.

In this highly competitive market, you need to be creative. If you want customers to pay attention, you need to give them something to pay attention to! If you have implemented Idea #45 (brainstorm with your staff), you've got some pretty good ideas for a promotion that will get your customers lining up to buy from you. This can be a discount on an annual service contract, a discount on consumable supplies, a customer appreciation sale, a buy-one-get-one deal... whatever will prod your customers into taking an immediate action. Stuck for an idea? Go back to your manufacturers and see what they are planning. Maybe they have promotional items you can use or a program they're planning to launch. Scour the Internet to look for ideas, both inside and outside your industry. Be innovative. Be creative. Be ready to do this *now!*

41. PURCHASE A LIST OF PROSPECTS.

You know the types of customers you want: their business types, buying habits, locations. Use this knowledge to purchase a list of prospects to expand your sales opportunities by pitching to new customers. Use this list to reach out with an enticing offer to drive them to your website and learn more about your business. Hit that touchpoint that grabs their attention. What is the common denominator about your competition that creates frustration among these customers? What can you offer that will set you apart from the rest? Use your thought leader reputation, repertoire of articles (Idea #35), success stories (#34), direct mail, website, email, and other events to touch them and win new business.

42. CREATE NICHE OFFERS.

Now that you have categorized your database (Idea #4), target a promotion to a specific segment of your customer list. Look at a segment in a certain industry or a group that has consistently purchased products within the same vertical market group. Use your understanding of these customers to develop specific offerings. Try collaborating with a business whose offerings complement yours. Create a promotional partnership with a tantalizing offer. For example, if you resell hardware, partner with a business that sells software. It's a win-win for you, your partner, and your customers!

43. UP-SELL OR CROSS-SELL YOUR CUSTOMERS.

One of the best ways to boost your sales quickly is to get your customers to buy deeper into your product line. This means up-selling them to a higher quantity than they ordinarily do (through volume incentives) or showing them the value of upgrading to a newer version. You can also cross-sell them to products that they haven't purchased from you (but should). Usually, the customer is just not made aware of the other products, perhaps stuck in a rut of buying what is familiar. Your job is to open their eyes to these products. And, since they're already comfortable buying from you, the deal closer is much easier, quicker, and probably more profitable than with a newcomer to your customer base. So, pick three customers today, get on the phone, and up- or cross-sell them.

Tune up your internal machine.

44. RE-EVALUATE YOUR COMPUTER SYSTEM.

Your own computer system is often like the tale of the cobbler's kids who have no shoes. You spend your days telling your customers about the latest tools they need to maximize their computer system but you don't take your own advice. Is your system doing what you need it to do? Ask your staff for input on features they'd like to have. Determine what you need and then look at what's available. Be sure to consider leasing, particularly if you upgrade your equipment every two or three years.

45. SCHEDULE A BRAINSTORMING SESSION WITH YOUR STAFF.

You never know where great ideas will come from. Every one of your team members brings a wealth of very unique, personal experience and knowledge. Bring them together once a month to brainstorm ideas to improve your business, better serve your customers, solve a problem, or come up with an idea for a special event or promotion. Maybe you can look for ways to find new business, get more business from your existing customers, or maximize the latest industry trend. Instead of using your role as The Boss, bring in an objective facilitator to ask questions and prompt the brainstorming. Set up your session in a casual environment that will promote creative thinking. And be sure to serve food and drinks to the group. Growling stomachs and thirsty mouths do not contribute to brain boosts!

46. GET A GOAL BUDDY.

We've all done it. Cheated on a diet. Given up on New Year's resolutions. Cancelled plans that get in the way of your daily grind. And
you get away with it, because you have no accountability. There are
no diet police or resolutions SWAT team checking up on you. Without a system of accountability, you can be absolutely positive that
your goals will not be met! But if you find pair up with the Goal
Buddy, you create a means to reaching your objective. Find someone
else who has goals to achieve. Share your goals and make yourselves
accountable by checking in with each other on a regular basis (at
least weekly). Ask your GB for an update on progress and be sure
your GB does the same to you. Share the challenges you are facing
and the obstacles that are holding you back. Together, you might
find solutions.

Dream!

47. SCHEDULE UNINTERRUPTED "VISION TIME".

Michael Gerber, author of the bestselling E-Myth business books, advises entrepreneurs to stop working at your business and start working on your business. Once a week, block out one to three hours on your calendar for "Vision Time". Get away from distractions (i.e., leave your office), turn off your email and cell phone, and put your mind to work on where you can take your business. By putting this activity on your schedule, you give yourself this permission to think freely and make a commitment to the vision of what you'd like your business to become.

48. MAKE A WISH LIST.

During your vision time, ask yourself, "How can I do better?" and "What more can I do for my customers?" Write down your answers in your note-taking system (see Ideas #1 and 2!). What would you like to do for yourself, your business, and your customers? Now ask yourself a few more questions. "What do I wish I could have in my product/service line?" "What would make my business stand out from the competition?" "What would I do for this business if I only had the time and/or resources to get it done?" During your scheduled Vision Time (see Idea #47), work on your wish list. Keep adding to it freely. Don't talk yourself out of wishes because those gentle reminders just might help you make them a reality.

49. MAKE ONE WISH COME TRUE.

Focus on just one item in your wish list and create a step-by-step plan to make your wish come true. What will you need to change? Do you need additional staff? What skills will be required? What equipment or other resources will you need? Whose help will be essential to making this work? Write down those steps and then start with the very first one today. Push yourself to complete as many as possible in one day. If that doesn't happen, set yourself a list of priorities for tomorrow, and the next day, and the next day. If you want that wish to become reality, you must remain focused on the steps to achieving that goal!

Start now!

50. PICK ONE OF THESE IDEAS EVERY DAY AND ACT ON IT!

Start with #1 and work your way through this list. Make a note of the results. For every idea that delivers for you, repeat it!!

Do you have an idea for improving your business that's not on this list? Share it with us for the next edition!

About the Author

 A dedicated marketing professional, Michelle Kabele has been helping technology companies develop award-winning channel partner programs and marketing strategies for over 10 years. Her innovative channel marketing concepts have been adopted and implemented by many leading technology companies, including Zebra Technologies, 3Com Corporation and U.S. Robotics. Moreover, Michelle has worked extensively with VARs throughout North America and thoroughly understands the realities and practicalities they in planning and executing effective promotional, marketing, and sales campaigns. Michelle has an MBA from the J.L. Kellogg Graduate School of Management (Evanston, Ill.) and an undergraduate degree from Northwestern University (Evanston, Ill.) She is the author of *Great Marketing is Free!*, *All the Web's A Stage*, and numerous marketing articles. She lives in suburban Chicago.

For more great ways to build your business,
check out Michelle Kabele's other ebooks:

Great Marketing Is Free!

All the Web's A Stage

*Just Say "Yes!": The Power of Creative
Thinking Outside That Tired Old Box*

Visit www.ideastorm.com for the most up-to-the-minute
news, advice, ideas, and just cool stuff.